ESSENTIAL
BIRDS

by Arnold Ringstad

CONTENT CONSULTANT
Kevin R. Burgio, PhD
Research Scientist
University of Connecticut

ESSENTIAL
ANIMALS

Essential Library

An Imprint of Abdo Publishing
abdobooks.com

abdobooks.com

Published by Abdo Publishing, a division of ABDO, PO Box 398166, Minneapolis, Minnesota 55439. Copyright © 2022 by Abdo Consulting Group, Inc. International copyrights reserved in all countries. No part of this book may be reproduced in any form without written permission from the publisher. Essential Library™ is a trademark and logo of Abdo Publishing.

Printed in the United States of America, North Mankato, Minnesota.
102021
012022

THIS BOOK CONTAINS RECYCLED MATERIALS

Cover Photos: Kotomiti Okuma/Shutterstock Images (penguin); Passakorn Umpornmaha/Shutterstock Images (macaw); Rostislav Stach/Shutterstock Images (mallard); Sari ONeal/Shutterstock Images (hummingbird); Shutterstock Images (puffin, flamingo)
Interior Photos: Shutterstock Images, 1, 6, 7 (top), 10, 32, 45, 48, 52, 58, 86, 89, 102 (penguin), 103 (chicken); Ryan M. Bolton/Shutterstock Images, 4; Guan Jiangchi/Shutterstock Images, 5; L. Galbraith/Shutterstock Images, 7 (second); Katalin Linda/Shutterstock Images, 7 (third); Milan Zygmunt/Shutterstock Images, 7 (fourth); Gordon Pusnik/Shutterstock Images, 7 (bottom); Christian Musat/Shutterstock Images, 9; Ondrej Prosicky/Shutterstock Images, 11, 94–95, 102 (macaw); Jennifer Bosvert/Shutterstock Images, 12, 102 (woodpecker); Hane Street/Shutterstock Images, 13; Mariusz Lopusiewicz/Shutterstock Images, 14; Francois Gohier/Science Source, 16; Vladimir Wrangel/Shutterstock Images, 18; M. Watson/Science Source, 19, 102 (condor); Arnold van Wijk/Shutterstock Images, 20, 102 (puffin); Eric Isselee/Shutterstock Images, 21 (left), 66–67; Kotomiti Okuma/Shutterstock Images, 21 (right); Rudmer Zwerver/Shutterstock Images, 22; Daria Nipot/Shutterstock Images, 24; Natalia Golovina/Shutterstock Images, 25; Jeroen Visser/Shutterstock Images, 26, 103 (pelican); MZ Photo CZ/Shutterstock Images, 28, 96, 98, 103 (albatross); Anan Kaewkhammul/Shutterstock Images, 29; Marc Freebrey/Shutterstock Images, 30, 103 (owl); Bob Kennett/Science Source, 33; Oleksandr Lytvynenko/Shutterstock Images, 34–35; Piotr Krzeslak/Shutterstock Images, 36, 41, 103 (crane), 103 (cuckoo); Gallinago Media/Shutterstock Images, 37; Muriel Hazan/Science Source, 38; Vishnevskiy Vasily/Shutterstock Images, 40, 42; John Navajo/Shutterstock Images, 43; Andrzej Kubik/Shutterstock Images, 44, 103 (ostrich); Lakeview Images/Shutterstock Images, 46; Anton Ivanov/Shutterstock Images, 47; Travel Media Productions/Shutterstock Images, 50, 51; Iliuta Goean/Shutterstock Images, 53, 102 (eagle); Tomas Hulik Artpoint/Shutterstock Images, 54; Zhecho Planinski/Shutterstock Images, 55; Volodymyr Burdiak/Shutterstock Images, 56, 103 (bustard); Frank McClintock/Shutterstock Images, 57; Gerald Cubitt/Science Source, 60, 103 (kiwi); Filip Bjorkman/Shutterstock Images, 62; Brent Stephenson/Nature Picture Library/Alamy, 63; Jesus Cobaleda/Shutterstock Images, 64, 103 (flamingo); John A. Anderson/Shutterstock Images, 65; Jiri Hrebicek/Shutterstock Images, 67; Jan Lindblad/Science Source, 68; Tomas Drahos/Shutterstock Images, 69, 102 (hoatzin); Anita Studer/Science Source, 70; Rachel Moon/Shutterstock Images, 72; Fabian Junge/Shutterstock Images, 73, 103 (sparrow); Vitaly Ilyasov/Shutterstock Images, 74; Thorsten Spoerlein/Shutterstock Images, 76, 102 (mallard); Jeffry Weymier/Shutterstock Images, 76–77; Brent Grieves/Shutterstock Images, 78; Steve Oehlenschlager/Shutterstock Images, 79; Leif Ingvarson/Shutterstock Images, 80, 102 (tropicbird); Marisa Estivill/Shutterstock Images, 81; Martin Mecnarowski/Shutterstock Images, 82; Imago History Collection/Alamy, 84; Helen J. Davies/Shutterstock Images, 85, 103 (pigeon); Jorge Alejandro Gonzalez/Shutterstock Images, 87; Steve Byland/Shutterstock Images, 88, 102 (hummingbird); Agnieszka Bacal/Shutterstock Images, 90; Alan Jeffery/Shutterstock Images, 92; Passakorn Umpornmaha/Shutterstock Images, 93; Hugh Lansdown/Shutterstock Images, 97; Red Line Editorial, 102–103 (map)

Editor: Katharine Hale
Series Designer: Sarah Taplin

Library of Congress Control Number: 2020949096

Publisher's Cataloging-in-Publication Data

Names: Ringstad, Arnold, author.
Title: Essential birds / by Arnold Ringstad
Description: Minneapolis, Minnesota : Abdo Publishing, 2022 | Series: Essential animals | Includes online resources and index.
Identifiers: ISBN 9781532195518 (lib. bdg.) | ISBN 9781098215897 (ebook)
Subjects: LCSH: Birds--Juvenile literature. | Birds--Behavior--Juvenile literature. | Animals--Identification--Juvenile literature. | Zoology--Juvenile literature.
Classification: DDC 598.2--dc23

CONTENTS

INTRODUCTION 4

ACORN WOODPECKER 12

ANDEAN CONDOR 16

ATLANTIC PUFFIN 20

AUSTRALIAN PELICAN 24

BARN OWL 28

CHICKEN 32

COMMON CRANE 36

COMMON CUCKOO 40

COMMON OSTRICH 44

EMPEROR PENGUIN 48

GOLDEN EAGLE 52

GREAT BUSTARD 56

GREAT SPOTTED KIWI 60

GREATER FLAMINGO 64

HOATZIN 68

HOUSE SPARROW 72

MALLARD 76

RED-BILLED TROPICBIRD 80

ROCK PIGEON 84

RUBY-THROATED HUMMINGBIRD 88

SCARLET MACAW 92

WANDERING ALBATROSS 96

ESSENTIAL FACTS   100   SOURCE NOTES   108
BIRDS AROUND THE WORLD   102   INDEX   110
GLOSSARY   104   ABOUT THE AUTHOR   112
ADDITIONAL RESOURCES   106   ABOUT THE CONSULTANT 112

INTRODUCTION

There are 13 species of finches, often called Darwin's Finches, on the Galápagos Islands.

Birds have captured the human imagination for thousands of years. People around the world have long drawn inspiration from these amazing flying animals, creating art and stories centered on the wonder of flight and the mythic power of birds. From the phoenix of ancient Rome to the thunderbird found in many Native American cultures including the Lakota, Ojibwe, and Arapaho cultures, birds have become creatures of legends.

Humanity found practical uses for birds too. People used birds and their eggs as sources of food, hunting some species and domesticating others. They turned feathers into decorations, clothing, arrows, and fishing lures. Quills became writing tools, and guano—or bird droppings—served as a useful fertilizer. Studying finches on the Galápagos Islands helped Charles Darwin develop the theory of evolution, laying the groundwork for modern biology.

In today's world, the routine nature of human flight may have made birds seem less magical. But for everyday people and scientists alike, birds continue to amaze. Millions of people participate in the hobby of bird-watching, using binoculars, cameras, and audio recorders to observe the birds around them. Some bird species are popular pets. Others are commonly hunted for sport. For the scientific community, birds provide a window into the past. Researchers believe that today's birds descended from dinosaurs. In fact, paleontologist Julia Clarke says, "Birds are living dinosaurs, just as we are mammals."[1]

BIRD BODIES

Birds make up one of the major branches of animal life on Earth. They are known for their ability to fly, but they are not the only animals that do this. Bats and many types of insects also evolved this skill. What makes birds unique is their feathers.

INTRODUCTION

Feathers are made up of keratin, a protein that is also found in reptile scales and mammal hairs. There are multiple types of feathers. Contour feathers cover most of the bird, helping to make it streamlined for flight. Beneath them are down feathers, which help to insulate the body. The contour feathers are typically shed and replaced at least once a year in a process called molting.

Like mammals, birds have four-chambered hearts. Their hearts are relatively large, in some species reaching 2.4 percent of their body weight, compared to a maximum of 0.8 percent in mammals. The paces of their heartbeats have a vast range. Ostrich hearts beat at a human-like 70 beats per minute. Hummingbird hearts can thump along at a staggering 1,000 beats per minute.[2]

Birds reproduce by laying hard-shell eggs rather than giving birth to live young. The developing

FUN FACT

Some birds possess a strong sense of smell. Turkey vultures have even been used to locate leaks in oil pipelines.

Ostrich eggs, *back*, quail eggs, *left*, and chicken eggs, *right*, are all different sizes.

INTRODUCTION

bird grows within the egg. An egg may seem delicate, but its oval shape gives it exceptional strength. The size of bird eggs can vary widely. A hummingbird egg might weigh as little as 0.007 ounces (0.2 g), while an ostrich egg tips the scales at more than 3 pounds (1.4 kg).[3]

Birds have many different beak shapes. This diversity is a result of adaptations to eating different types of foods. Woodpeckers' pointed beaks peck into tree bark so the birds can feed on the insects inside. Hawks and eagles use their sharp, hook-shaped beaks to tear prey into pieces. A duck's flat bill contains tooth-like structures that filter food from water.

BEAK SHAPES

DUCK
Flat with edges that filter food from water

EAGLE
Hooked to tear flesh

FINCH
Strong and cone-shaped to crack seeds

HUMMINGBIRD
Long and thin to extend into flowers and drink nectar

WOODPECKER
Strong and pointed to chisel holes in trees

Bird beaks are shaped differently based on each bird's diet.

Another key feature of birds is their exceptional vision. They have large eyes relative to their bodies. This makes their visual sense sharper, which is important for flying and hunting. For example, an eagle has eyeballs nearly the size of a human's. But the eagle can see much farther. Researchers estimate it can spot a rabbit at a range of more than three miles (4.8 km).[4]

BIRD BEHAVIORS

The ability to fly is the single best-known characteristic of birds. Most bird species are able to fly. Key adaptations, including lightweight skeletons and the development of winged forelimbs, have made this possible. In general, the birds that can fly do so by flapping their wings to gain altitude and speed, steering with their tails.

The specifics of flying differ significantly between various types of birds. Albatrosses gracefully soar on ocean breezes with long, narrow wings. Chickens beat their short, wide wings rapidly to fly short distances. Birds such as robins and cardinals zip from perch to perch on short, rounded wings. Hummingbirds beat their narrow, curved wings extremely quickly, allowing them to hover in place.

Flight is not the only way birds get around. Many mix flying with walking or swimming. And some birds

BIRD EXTREMES

The thousands of bird species vary greatly in their physical forms. The bird with the widest wingspan is the wandering albatross. Its wings stretch 11.5 feet (3.5 m) from tip to tip. The heaviest flying bird is the trumpeter swan, which can weigh 37 pounds (17 kg). Flightless birds grow much heavier; the largest is the ostrich at more than 330 pounds (150 kg). On the other end of the spectrum, the smallest living bird is the bee hummingbird. It measures approximately 2.5 inches (6.3 cm) long and weighs around 0.1 ounce (3 g), or a bit less than a nickel.[5]

INTRODUCTION

have completely lost the ability to fly. Instead, they have evolved to move in different ways. Ostriches developed long, powerful legs and can sprint at 43 miles per hour (69 kmh). Penguins' wings act as effective flippers, allowing some species to dive to depths of more than 1,500 feet (460 m).

Birds are also known for the noises they make. Among the most common of these is birdsong, or noises that are often made to attract a mate. These songs can vary between individuals, and researchers think birds may be able to specifically identify one another through song. Bird behavior includes other kinds of noises too. Noises called location notes help birds stay together in groups. Birds use alarm notes to warn others of danger nearby. Young birds use begging calls to request food from their parents.

The use of eggs to reproduce leads to another notable bird behavior: nesting. Most bird species create nests where they lay eggs and incubate them until the eggs hatch. Some birds simply dig a hole in the ground. Others use a crack or crevice in a tree or rock. Many birds construct nests of varying complexity out of materials such as sticks or leaves.

INTRODUCTION

Birds lay as few as one egg and as many as 20. The incubation period ranges from 11 to 80 days. In some species, the young leave the nest shortly after hatching. In others, parents raise their young in or near the nest for eight months or more.

CLASSIFYING BIRDS

Scientists classify life in a series of increasingly specific groups. From broadest to narrowest, these groups are kingdom, phylum, class, order, family, genus, and species. Birds are part of the kingdom Animalia, which includes all animals. They are part of the phylum Chordata, which is made up mostly of vertebrates. The class Aves contains all birds.

Within Aves, birds are divided into approximately 25 orders. The exact number depends on which classification system is used; scientists disagree on how to organize some of the orders. By far the largest order is Passeriformes, also known as perching birds. It contains about 5,700 species, or more than half of all birds. Sparrows, cardinals, ravens, and many others are in this order. Other major orders include Apodiformes (approximately 435 species, including hummingbirds), Piciformes (about 400 species, including woodpeckers), Psittaciformes (approximately 400 species, including parrots), and Charadriiformes (about 370 species, including gulls). Overall, there are more than 10,400 known living bird species.[6] Each species has a scientific name made up of its genus and species. For example, the Pacific gull's scientific name is *Larus pacificus*.

ESSENTIAL BIRDS

This book presents 22 notable bird species from around the world. The species are presented alphabetically by their common names. These birds represent the amazing diversity of appearance and behavior in the class Aves. They range in size from the tiny ruby-throated hummingbird to the enormous common ostrich. Some, such as the house sparrow, are seen commonly in everyday life. Others, such as the emperor penguin, live only in remote places. Each species plays an important role in its ecosystem. Narrative stories, colorful photos, fact boxes, and the latest scientific findings help bring to life the flying animals that have been inspiring people throughout human history.

Toucans belong to the order Piciformes.

ACORN WOODPECKER

Acorn woodpeckers stuff acorns in holes the birds have drilled into trees.

In the woodlands of coastal central California, a series of short, sharp thumps echoes among the trees. The acorn woodpeckers are hard at work. Several of the birds cling to the side of a bare, dried-out tree. Their heads rhythmically beat the wood, occasionally pause briefly, then resume. The woodpeckers are contributing to a project that their group has been working on for generations. Arrayed across the face of the tree are thousands of holes.

Each hole has been excavated one peck at a time, a process that scientists estimate may take roughly an hour. A typical woodpecker group might create a few hundred holes per year. This granary tree has been decades in the making.[7]

ACORN WOODPECKER

A closer look reveals that each hole contains an acorn. Suddenly a new woodpecker arrives, spreading its black-and-white wings wide as it finds a spot where it can cling to the tree. It carries a fat-rich acorn in its beak. Once the bird settles into place, it stuffs the acorn into a completed hole. Then it hammers the acorn in securely with its beak. Working together, these woodpeckers are ensuring that their group will have enough food for winter.

FUN FACT

The largest granary tree ever observed had approximately 50,000 holes. Scientists estimate it took more than 100 years to construct.[8]

ACORN WOODPECKER

APPEARANCE AND HABITAT

The acorn woodpecker has mostly black feathers and white feathers. There is often a yellow hue along the throat, but the most striking coloring is the bird's red crown. Examining the woodpecker's crown reveals an individual's sex. In females, a black band separates the red crown from the white feathers of the forehead. In males, the red and white areas meet.

Acorn woodpeckers live only in the Americas. In the United States, they can be found in the western areas of Oregon and California, in the border region between Arizona and New Mexico, and in a small patch of western Texas. They live in much of Mexico, as well as in a few areas in Central America. Populations of the birds also live in the woodland slopes of the Andes Mountains in Colombia. Within these regions, the common thread is that acorn woodpeckers live in habitats with the oak trees that provide their acorns. Those include oak woodlands, but they also include other types of forests as long as oaks are nearby. The birds can live in urban or suburban areas with oaks too.

GRANARIES

Acorn woodpeckers eat a variety of foods. They hunt insects, including flying ants and related species.

14

The birds eat fruits, seeds, flower nectar, and tree sap. They will also hunt small animals, such as lizards, bats, mice, and even other birds. But they are best known for the food that gives them their name: acorns.

The storage of acorns in trees is unique to the acorn woodpecker. The trees they use are known as granaries. A granary may have just a few holes, or it may have thousands. A group of woodpeckers, which contains up to a dozen birds, typically has one primary granary and one or more secondary granaries. The birds drill their holes in winter, usually in dead branches or areas with thick bark. This avoids harming living trees. The holes are mainly used for acorns, but the birds will store almonds, walnuts, or pecans when they are available. They will also drink from the holes when water collects inside.

Once a granary is established, the acorn woodpeckers guard it fiercely. A tree full of acorns is a tempting target for squirrels, crows, or fellow woodpeckers. A group will use a behavior called mobbing, repeatedly diving at the invading animal to defend the granary. This is often successful at driving away the would-be thief.

ACORN WOODPECKER
Melanerpes formicivorus

SIZE
Wingspan of 1.2–1.4 feet (35–43 cm)

WEIGHT
2.3–3.2 ounces (65–90 g)

RANGE
United States, Mexico, Central America, Colombia

HABITAT
Oak woodlands, other forests, areas near rivers

DIET
Acorns, insects, sap, fruits, small animals

LIFE SPAN
9.5 years on average

ANDEAN CONDOR

Andean condors scavenge on dead animals.

High in the air, among mountain peaks, an Andean condor soars atop the air currents. His broad black, white, and gray wings hold him aloft on the warm air currents generated by the midday sun. Only occasionally does he need to beat his wings to maintain flight. The condor's sharp yellow eyes scan the grasslands below. He is looking for his next meal.

On the distant ground there is a dead guanaco, a llama-like South American mammal. It appears to have been here for some time; other animals have been picking at the carrion. The Andean condor trains his eyes on the carcass and begins his descent. He arrives on the ground hungry. Smaller scavengers clear out as the enormous condor approaches.

The condor begins ripping skin and flesh off the carrion with his hooked beak, and other condors begin to arrive for the feast. They share the guanaco. Each bird eats its fill. The male eats so much he will be unable to fly for a while.

HIGH FLYER

The Andean condor is the largest raptor in the world, and it is the biggest flying bird of South America. Among all South American birds, only the ostrich-like rhea is larger.[9] The condor mainly lives in the Andes Mountains along the continent's western edge, high above grasslands and alpine areas. It sometimes searches for food in lowland deserts and along the shoreline too.

FUN FACT

The Andean condor is the national bird of multiple South American countries, including Bolivia, Chile, Colombia, and Ecuador.

The condor belongs to a group of birds known as the New World vultures. There are vultures in Africa too, but the New World vultures are more closely related to storks. The Andean condor is the only New World vulture that shows sexual dimorphism, meaning that there are differences in appearance between males and females. The male has a large, fleshy crest called a comb atop his head. The female lacks this feature. The difference can also be seen in the eyes: males have yellow eyes, while females have red ones.

The condor can soar for hours at high altitudes with minimal energy use, taking advantage of warm currents of rising air known as thermals. It uses its broad wings to catch these updrafts and fly from one thermal to the next. It may have to flap its wings only once per hour. Feathers at the tips of the wings point slightly upward, reducing drag and extending flying time. Some airplane wings use a similar design for efficient flight.

SCAVENGING

Among the most notable behaviors of the Andean condor is the way it eats: scavenging. It soars high above the ground, keeping an eye out for dead mammals below. The condor will feed on dead guanacos and livestock. When it scavenges near the shore, it may eat marine mammals, sharks, or seabirds. Scavenging keeps the ecosystem healthier. By eating dead

animals before they begin to decay, condors prevent the spread of disease.

One immediately noticeable feature of the Andean condor is its bald head. This adaptation is useful when scavenging. While feeding, the condor may need to put its head inside a rotting carcass. Having a bare head means that the prey's flesh is unable to stick to the condor's feathers, keeping the bird cleaner and preventing potential infections.

ANDEAN CONDOR
Vultur gryphus

SIZE
Wingspan of 8.5–10.5 feet (2.6–3.2 m)

WEIGHT
Female 18–24 pounds (8–11 kg); male 24–33 pounds (11–15 kg)

RANGE
South America, in the Andes Mountains and along the western coastline

HABITAT
Mountains, grasslands, lowland deserts, shorelines

DIET
Scavenges large mammals, including guanacos, livestock, marine mammals

LIFE SPAN
About 50 years maximum in the wild

ATLANTIC PUFFIN

The rocky shoreline in the North Atlantic teems with Atlantic puffins. Their red-tipped bills and orange legs and feet create splashes of bright color against the slate-gray rock and patchy areas of mosses and grasses. The birds mill around, entering and exiting small burrows excavated into the thin soil. A few of their beaks are still caked with dirt from digging. Inside the burrows are small, puffy, black-feathered chicks. They are hungry.

A puffin parent flies out to sea and lands on the water. It swims around on the surface, holding its wings against its body and paddling its feet. Occasionally it dips its head below the water to look around. It is watching for a school of small fish known as sand lances. Suddenly, the puffin spots its prey. It dives beneath the waves, spreading its wings wide and beating them as if it were flying. The puffin slices through the

A group of puffins is called a colony.

water, directly through the school of sand lances. It emerges from the water with a dozen of them in its mouth. They'll make a good meal for its baby puffin back at the colony.

PUFFIN BASICS

The Atlantic puffin belongs to a family of birds known as auks. The tops of puffins' bodies are covered in black feathers, while their undersides are white. This plain coloring contrasts sharply with their triangular bills, which take on hues of red, yellow, orange, and gray. The colors become bolder during mating season.

PUFFINS VS. PENGUINS

PUFFINS
- Wings capable of flight
- Live in the Northern Hemisphere
- Weigh around one pound (0.45 kg)

PENGUINS
- Wings used only for swimming
- Live in the Southern Hemisphere
- Can weigh more than 60 pounds (27 kg)

SIMILARITIES
Black-and-white coloring • Eat small fish

Puffins and penguins look somewhat similar, and people often confuse them for each other. But these birds are not closely related. They live in different places and have different lifestyles.

ATLANTIC PUFFIN

The puffin makes its home along the shorelines of the North Atlantic, a vast range encompassing Maine, eastern Canada, western Greenland, and the coasts of northern Europe. During the breeding season it lives in large colonies that may contain thousands of individuals. The birds seek places where they can lay their eggs, either in excavated burrows in the soil or in naturally occurring crevices in the rock. Each female typically lays one egg per year. The spectacle of these huge colonies attracts human attention, and some colonies have become tourist destinations.

DIVING AND HUNTING

Atlantic puffins are awkward when walking or flying, but they

FUN FACT

Atlantic puffins commonly carry approximately ten fish in their mouths at once. But the largest observed number was a single puffin carrying an incredible 62 fish.[10]

demonstrate impressive agility underwater. Their wings allow them to glide smoothly through the water on hunting dives, with their feet acting as rudders to help them steer. The birds typically dive to a maximum depth of approximately 230 feet (70 m), and one study found that the average dive lasted about 28 seconds.[11]

The puffins feed on small fish that congregate in schools, including sand lances, haddock, herring, and others, diving directly into the schools. If they are hunting for themselves, they will eat the fish underwater. If they are bringing food back to the colony, they will hold multiple fish tightly in their beaks. A special adaptation makes this easier: there are backward-pointing spines on both the roof of the mouth and the tongue to firmly secure the caught fish.

Much of what is known about puffins comes from observing them in the breeding season in the spring and summer. When the birds disperse from their colonies in the fall, they fly out to sea, returning in the spring. Scientists know relatively little about the birds' lives during this period away from the colonies.

ATLANTIC PUFFIN
Fratercula arctica

SIZE
Wingspan of 1.8–2 feet (53–61 cm)

WEIGHT
0.7–1.2 pounds (0.3–0.6 kg)

RANGE
North Atlantic Ocean; coasts of northern Europe, eastern Canada, western Greenland, Iceland, Maine

HABITAT
Rocky shorelines and open ocean

DIET
Small schooling fish, including sand lances, haddock, herring

LIFE SPAN
About 32 years maximum in the wild

AUSTRALIAN PELICAN

Pelicans often feed in groups, working together to catch fish.

A thousand Australian pelicans are gathered on the crystal-blue water along the Australian coast. Other than an occasional hiss or groan, they make little noise. They are focused on the task at hand. Beneath them is a massive school of fish. Each of the pelicans is doing its part, moving its bill or beating its wings to drive the fish into an ever-shrinking circle.

Finally, the school of fish forms a dense mass at the center of the pelicans, and it's feeding time. A pelican thrusts its head into the churning waters. A hook on the end of its bill grips a fish, and the pelican opens wide. The fish and the water around it fill the stretchy pouch in the pelican's lower bill. The pelican tucks its pouch in toward its chest, draining the water. It moves its bill around until the fish's head is pointed down the pelican's throat. Then, with a swift jerk, the pelican swallows the fish whole.

APPEARANCE

The Australian pelican is mostly white, with black feathers on its wings, back, and tail. Males tend to be larger than females, but the coloring is the same between the sexes. The pelican's eyes are brown, encircled with a yellow eye ring. Its short legs and large webbed feet are gray. At up to 1.6 feet (50 cm) long, its pale-pink bill is the longest of any living bird.[12] The tip of the upper bill has a yellow-and-orange point that may be used to catch

FUN FACT
Australian pelicans have been observed holding their bills open to collect rainwater for drinking.

slippery prey. The bottom bill includes the pelican's trademark feature: a flexible pouch known as the gular pouch. It can stretch to hold up to three gallons (11.4 L) of water.

These bill features help the Australian pelican eat the fish that are its primary food source, including carp and perch. The birds have also been known to eat crustaceans, such as shrimp and crayfish, as well as insects, reptiles, and even other birds. Enormous flocks of hundreds of pelicans hunt cooperatively, driving fish into confined areas before feasting. An Australian pelican feeds similarly to other pelican species, tilting its head forward and then thrusting its bill underwater to grab a meal.

HABITATS

As its name suggests, the Australian pelican is mostly found in Australia, including the island of Tasmania. It also lives in Indonesia and Papua New Guinea. It has also been spotted in New Zealand, Fiji, and other regional islands. These journeys are likely aided by its ability to fly long distances. Soaring between warm updrafts, the pelican has been known to remain aloft for 24 hours at a time.

The pelican lives in habitats with plentiful open water, whether coastal or inland. Along the coast, it makes its home along the shore, in inlets, or on offshore islands. Away from the sea, it lives on lakes and rivers. Wherever they are, Australian pelicans are highly social birds. In addition to their cooperative feeding, they fly together in groups and breed in enormous colonies that can include up to 40,000 individual birds.[13]

AUSTRALIAN PELICAN
Pelecanus conspicillatus

SIZE
Wingspan of 7.6–8.2 feet (2.3–2.5 m)

WEIGHT
9–15 pounds (4–7 kg)

RANGE
Australia, Indonesia, Papua New Guinea, Solomon Islands, East Timor, Fiji, New Zealand

HABITAT
Areas of open water, including coastlines, inlets, lakes, rivers

DIET
Mostly fish, but also crustaceans, reptiles, birds, insects

LIFE SPAN
15–25 years in the wild; maximum 50 years in captivity

BARN OWL

The barn owl's excellent hearing and sharp talons make it a fearsome predator.

As the sun sets over the Oregon horizon, the small town's church steeple is silhouetted starkly against a hazy orange sky. Inside the steeple is a sleeping barn owl. Soon daylight gives way to twilight and eventually darkness. The owl awakens. With clouds rolling in and obscuring the moon, it is a pitch-black night. But that is no obstacle for the hungry owl's hunt.

The owl glides down silently from the tall steeple, its deep, slow wingbeats making virtually no noise. Any mice in the thick grass below are completely unaware of its presence. The barn owl has sharp vision, but in darkness this deep, it relies on its excellent hearing to hunt. It flies low over the field until it zeroes in on the distinct sound of a scurrying mouse. The owl extends its long legs and talons, swooping noiselessly toward the mouse. It reaches through the long grass and seizes its next meal.

APPEARANCE

The barn owl is typically medium-sized compared to other owls. Its face is covered by a heart-shaped ruff, and its long, featherless legs allow it to reach into tall grass to grab its prey. Its top side is gold colored with black-and-white markings. The color of its underside can vary, ranging from unmarked white to a yellowish brown with darker spots.

The size and coloring of the barn owl differ widely across its enormous range. It is not only among the most widely distributed owls but also among the most widely distributed land birds of any kind. It has been spotted on every continent except Antarctica. Across that broad geographic span, scientists

BARN OWL

Barn owls have such sensitive hearing that they also possess small, feathered flaps that can block sound if the environment is too loud.

recognize approximately 30 unique subspecies.[14]

The barn owl prefers to live in open spaces where it can hunt, meaning it usually avoids areas with mountains or dense forests. Grasslands, farmers' fields, and deserts are typical habitats, though it can also

FUN FACT
Barn owls are often monogamous, commonly mating for life.

be found in or near cities. It sometimes builds its nest in naturally occurring spaces, such as cliffs and caves, but it also nests in human structures. These include church steeples and the barns that give the owl its name.

STEALTHY HUNTER

Multiple adaptations make the barn owl a fearsome hunter. It has excellent vision, including in dim conditions after sunset. However, the owl's hearing is even better, allowing it to hunt in total darkness. Its ears are placed asymmetrically on its head, enhancing its ability to accurately determine where sounds originate. This lets the owl detect prey that is obscured by plants or snow.

The barn owl has incredible hearing, but it makes virtually no sound of its own that would warn its prey. Its rounded wings are large relative to its body, and it flies with deep, slow wingbeats. Downy feathers and a jagged leading edge on the bird's flight feathers help to silence the flight even further. These factors mean that the swooping flight of the barn owl causes little air disturbance, so it can sneak up silently on its small mammalian prey.

BARN OWL
Tyto alba

SIZE
Wingspan of 3.5–3.6 feet (1.07–1.1 m)

WEIGHT
0.9–1.4 pounds (0.4–0.6 kg)

RANGE
Every continent except Antarctica

HABITAT
Open areas, both rural and urban

DIET
Mostly small mammals, including mice, voles, shrews, rabbits

LIFE SPAN
1.75 years on average in the wild

CHICKEN

Chickens are raised on farms for meat and eggs.

The white chicken walks with short, quick steps across the green field. Its pale-yellow legs and broad feet steady the heavy bird on the dewy grass. The chicken is surrounded by hundreds of other birds of the same size, shape, and coloring. Chirps, clucks, and the rustling of feathers combine to create a background noise of busy activity.

Living on a free-range chicken farm in rural England, these birds are destined for the meat department of a British supermarket. For now, though, they wander between the field and a large chicken shed. In the shed, they can find food and water, along with wooden blocks to peck and perches to leap upon for exercise.

The experiences of chickens on this farm are not universal. Most domesticated chickens are raised in larger-scale factory farming operations, where they live in conditions that are more crowded and less sanitary. Others are raised in backyards as pets or for their eggs. As a domesticated bird, the chicken has been shaped by human activity and choices over the past several millennia.

CHICKEN ORIGINS

The animal we now call the chicken is mainly descended from the wild red jungle fowl (*Gallus gallus*), a bird that originated in India. This bird looks similar to modern chickens. In its natural habitat, the wild red jungle fowl eats insects, seeds, and fruits it finds on the forest floor. It can fly only short distances, launching itself upward into the trees to nest at night. Scientists believe that the gray jungle fowl, which comes from southern India, and other related species also contributed to the modern domesticated chicken.

Evidence suggests that independent groups of people domesticated

The wild red jungle fowl is an ancestor of the domesticated chicken.

the wild red jungle fowl in Southeast Asia starting approximately 7,400 years ago. It remained a regional species for thousands of years before it began spreading across the rest of the world about 2,000 years ago.[15] Following this dispersal, it became a common part of farms in Europe, Asia, and Africa.

MODERN CHICKENS

It was not until the early 1900s that chicken meat and eggs became the mass-produced products seen today. Large factory farms began using stacked cages in large facilities, carefully controlling conditions to maximize the output of poultry. A key breakthrough was that farmers learned to add antibiotics and vitamins to their chicken feed. Their chickens no longer had to go outdoors, where they would need sunlight to produce vitamin D. This method of farming spread in the United Kingdom after approximately 1920 and in the United States after 1945.

At first, meat was a relatively small portion of the domesticated chicken industry. Chickens were mainly used to lay eggs. If a chicken could no longer produce eggs, it would be slaughtered and used

FUN FACT

In ancient Rome, generals would watch how their chickens behaved before large battles. If the chickens ate well, it supposedly foretold a victory.

CHICKEN

as meat. But by the mid-1900s, meat became the more popular use for chickens. In the early 1990s, chicken became the most-eaten meat in the United States, passing beef in the rankings. In 2018, the average American ate approximately 94 pounds (43 kg) of chicken over the course of the year.[16]

CHICKEN
Gallus gallus domesticus

SIZE
2.3 feet (70 cm) tall on average

WEIGHT
5.7 pounds (2.6 kg) on average

RANGE
Domesticated worldwide

HABITAT
Domesticated on farms and in backyards

DIET
Chicken feed, made up mainly of grains

LIFE SPAN
Industrial chickens typically up to 3 years; free-range chickens up to 8 years; chickens in captivity up to 30 years

COMMON CRANE

The common crane gets a running start before taking flight.

The crisp Scandinavian air is getting colder by the day. Instinctually, the common crane knows it is time to go. It takes a few tentative steps with its long, thin legs. Then it leans its head forward and begins to accelerate with broad, loping strides. The crane extends its wings to the sides and flaps them in deep strokes. Each step becomes lighter as its wings start to catch the air. Finally the crane stretches its feet back behind its body. It is airborne, and its thousand-mile journey has begun.

Other cranes join this one in the air, forming a huge V shape made up of hundreds of individuals. As they fly to the southwest, passing over Germany, France, and Spain

COMMON CRANE

far below, the weather gradually warms. Occasionally the flock descends onto cropland, feeding on grains and potatoes left over after the harvest. Some birds continue on to Portugal and even Morocco, finding temperate lands in which to spend the winter. In spring they will make the reverse journey, returning north to breed.

APPEARANCE AND RANGE

The common crane is the largest bird living in Europe, with a wingspan stretching up to approximately 6.6 feet (2 m).[17] Its long legs and neck stretch out straight from its body while flying, giving it a sleek appearance in flight. The crane has a mostly slate-gray body, with a darker head that features a white stripe behind the eye. Atop its head is a distinct red patch.

The crane breeds in many places across Europe and Asia, including Scandinavia, north central China, eastern Russia, and Turkey. It winters to the south of these places, including in France, Spain, North Africa, southeastern China, the Middle East, Pakistan, and India. Within these diverse geographic locations, the

FUN FACT

The common crane can be distinguished in flight from a similar bird, the grey heron. The heron's neck is folded into an S shape, while the crane sticks its neck straight out.

37

COMMON CRANE

Flying in a V shape reduces wind resistance.

crane prefers to live in wetlands. The shallow water gives it a safe place to nest, and it is able to hunt for food in the surrounding fields. The common crane is omnivorous, eating roots, stems, and seeds along with worms, snails, and insects. It sometimes also eats small vertebrates, such as frogs, snakes, and fish. The crane hunts these by skewering them with its sharp beak.

RAISING THE YOUNG

Building nests in the water helps the crane defend its young from predators. After the female crane lays eggs, the parents alternate sitting on them to keep them warm. The eggs hatch in approximately 28 days. A few days after that, chicks are able to walk away from the nest with the parents to find food. A young crane's first flight typically happens at about ten weeks.

When it comes time to migrate in the fall, the crane family moves together. Young cranes learn not only the migration route but also safe places to stop, rest, and feed along the way. They learn to fly in V-shaped formations, taking turns in the lead to reduce wind resistance on birds behind them. This migration knowledge is passed from generation to generation.

COMMON CRANE
Grus grus

SIZE
Wingspan of 5.9–6.6 feet (1.8–2 m)

WEIGHT
9.9–13.5 pounds (4.5–6.1 kg)

RANGE
Breeds in northern areas of Europe, Russia, and China; winters in southern areas of Europe and Asia, and in North Africa

HABITAT
Shallow wetlands

DIET
Omnivorous, including roots, stems, seeds, invertebrates, frogs, lizards, fish

LIFE SPAN
More than 25 years in the wild; up to 40 years in captivity

COMMON CUCKOO

A baby cuckoo uses the scooped divot in its back to push rival eggs out of the nest.

The garden warbler's nest sits in a low bush in the German countryside. The nest's grasses, leaves, and roots support a batch of white eggs spotted with brown markings. One of the eggs rustles as it begins to hatch. But the bird that emerges is not a garden warbler. It is a common cuckoo. The other eggs sit motionless in the nest.

Before long, the young cuckoo's instincts kick in. It uses its back to shove the remaining eggs out of the nest, and they crack on the ground below. When the garden warbler parents return, they begin feeding the cuckoo, the only living chick in their nest. The chick continually calls out for food. In just a few weeks it has grown larger than the parents. Yet they continue to bring it a feast of insects.

By the end of the summer, the cuckoo is able to fly on its own. It departs for its winter home in Africa. Next year it will return to the same area, where it will attempt to deposit one of its own eggs in the nest of another bird.

CUCKOO BASICS

The common cuckoo has a gray top and a white underside with black bars. The female has a reddish tint to the upper chest area. The cuckoo's tail is dark brown with a white tip. Males are slightly larger than females.

FUN FACT

The common cuckoo can eat poisonous hairy caterpillars that most birds avoid. It bites one end off the caterpillar, then shakes it with its beak to get the poison out.

The cuckoo has a vast range spanning most of Europe and Asia. The birds fly south to warmer areas for the winter. For example, those in Europe generally migrate to sub-Saharan Africa. Those in Asia fly to the Philippines or Southeast Asia. The common cuckoo lives in a diverse array of habitats across this range, including forests, woodlands, marshes, and agricultural lands.

The diet of the cuckoo mainly consists of invertebrates. Caterpillars make up the largest share of its food, though it also consumes dragonflies, crickets, beetles, and spiders. It eats the larvae of these creatures as well as the adults.

BROOD PARASITISM

The cuckoo is notable for exhibiting a behavior known as brood parasitism. A female cuckoo will lay her egg in the nest of another bird species, known as the host, while the host is away. Cuckoo eggs commonly have colors or patterns matching those of the host species'.

The cuckoo egg generally hatches before those of the host. As the first to hatch, it soon gets fed by the host.

CUCKOO EGG

The young cuckoo gains strength, and it works to remove the rival eggs. It pushes against the eggs with its back, using its legs to ease them up and over the edge of the nest. If any of the host's eggs have already hatched, the cuckoo will push the rival chicks out too.

The host parents continue feeding the growing cuckoo. It becomes larger than them before it is able to live on its own, so keeping up with feeding it is a challenge. Eventually the cuckoo matures enough to fly and departs south on its migration.

COMMON CUCKOO
Cuculus canorus

SIZE
1.1 feet (33.5 cm) long on average

WEIGHT
3.8 ounces (108 g) on average

RANGE
Europe and Asia; migrates south to sub-Saharan Africa and Southeast Asia in the winter

HABITAT
Almost anywhere

DIET
Insects and other invertebrates

LIFE SPAN
12.9 years maximum in the wild

COMMON OSTRICH

Ostriches rely on their speed to escape predators, as they cannot fly.

The dry, grassy landscape is broken up by occasional shrubs. Two ostriches stride along on slender, muscular legs. Their eyes are alert for danger around them. One of them notices a cheetah standing motionless in the tall grass. The big cat's golden coat and small spots help it blend in against the background.

Suddenly the cheetah begins moving, starting slowly but accelerating quickly as its strides lengthen. The ostriches take notice, and they too begin to run. But one of them detected the danger slightly later, and it begins to lag behind. The cheetah zeroes in on the slower ostrich. Another cheetah emerges from the grass. Together they leap onto the ostrich, dragging it to the savanna floor. The bird tries to kick them with its powerful legs, but it is no use. It has become these cheetahs' next meal. The other ostrich is far away by now. It lives to run another day.

THE LARGEST BIRD

The ostrich is the largest bird in the world by weight, growing as heavy as 330 pounds (150 kg).[18] Its size makes it too heavy to fly. Instead, it uses its powerful legs to propel its bulk across the ground at high speeds. In a sprint it can reach 43 miles per hour (69 kmh).[19]

COMMON OSTRICH

Its flexible joints and tendons store energy, helping make such performance possible.

The body of a male ostrich is covered in black feathers, while the wings and tail are white. A thin ring of white feathers circles the neck, and most of the head and neck are bare. Female ostriches have similar coloring but duller, with more grays and browns.

FUN FACT

Ostriches may lie flat on the ground with their necks outstretched to avoid being seen by predators. They do not bury their heads in the sand.

WHERE OSTRICHES LIVE

Ostriches once lived in southwestern Asia, in Arabia, and across Africa. When their feathers became desirable items in the 1700s, heavy hunting nearly wiped them out. The development of ostrich farms in the 1800s eased this problem, but the birds' range had narrowed considerably. Today wild ostriches are confined to sub-Saharan Africa.

Ostriches make their homes in dry, open spaces, including deserts, savannas, and woodlands. They have adapted to need relatively little water, helping them survive in these arid areas. The birds eat mainly plants, including grasses, seeds, and the succulents common in dry places.

Ostrich feathers are commonly used in fans.

46

OSTRICH GROUPS

During the breeding season, ostriches form flocks that may contain up to 50 birds. A flock's territory covers up to 5.8 square miles (15 sq km). The birds are commonly found near grazing mammals, such as antelope and zebras. Rather than build nests, they scrape holes in the soil or sand for their eggs. Their shiny, white eggs measure six inches (15 cm) long by five inches (13 cm) wide and weigh approximately three pounds (1.4 kg).

Some ostrich flocks use communal nests, which can contain as many as 60 eggs. The eggs hatch in about 40 days. Running speed is key to an ostrich's defense, so the young must develop this skill quickly. At one month old, the chicks are capable of sprinting at 35 miles per hour (56 kmh).

COMMON OSTRICH
Struthio camelus

SIZE
5.75–9 feet (1.75–2.75 m) tall

WEIGHT
198–330 pounds (90–150 kg)

RANGE
Sub-Saharan Africa

HABITAT
Savannas, grasslands

DIET
Mostly plants, including grasses, seeds, succulents

LIFE SPAN
30–40 years in the wild; 50 years in captivity

EMPEROR PENGUIN

A penguin chick can stay in its father's brood pouch until it is one month old.

The female emperor penguin waddles off on her long journey to the sea to feed. Left behind on the icy, craggy breeding grounds are hundreds of other penguins—among them her mate. He holds their single egg in a fold of skin near his feet. The male penguin prepares to hunker down for nine frigid weeks while the egg incubates.

Meanwhile, the female completes her miles-long journey to the ocean. She dives deep to snatch fish, crustaceans, and squid, using her stiff wings as flippers to glide through the water. She remains underwater for minutes at a time. The penguin feeds and regains her strength after the stresses of laying the egg and going on her long journey.

When she returns home to the colony, she calls out to her mate. They use this call to find one other. The egg hatched while she was away. The tiny baby penguin has the first hints of gray feathers on its otherwise bare body.

The male penguin looks different than before. He has lost approximately 40 percent of his body mass after going months without food. Now it is his turn to feed. The female takes over caring for the baby, regurgitating food for it to eat. The male waddles off on his own long journey to the sea.

FUN FACT

The longest recorded dive by an emperor penguin lasted 21.8 minutes.[20]

ANTARCTIC BIRDS

Emperor penguins are the largest penguins. They are flightless, using their wings for swimming. Their coloring is mostly black and white, though they have patches of orange and yellow on their heads and breasts. The penguin's thin, curved beak has pink-orange stripes on its underside.

Antarctica is the only place where emperor penguins live. The temperatures there can dip to –40 degrees Fahrenheit (–40°C) in the winter. To survive, penguins have developed

Unable to fly, penguins waddle, slide on their bellies, and swim to get around.

several adaptations. They huddle together in groups of as many as 6,000 birds to stay warm and conserve energy. Penguins may also lie flat to reduce their exposure to the powerful, chilly winds that blow across Antarctica's coast.

Minimizing heat loss is especially important for males as they try to endure the long incubation period. The birds remain almost motionless for days in a row. They tuck their heads into their chests and pull their wings against their bodies. They rest with only their heels and tails touching the ground, minimizing contact with the cold surface.

MATING

Penguins mate monogamously within a breeding season, meaning each bird has just one mate. But emperor penguins may change mates from year to year. Males and females use vocal calls during a courtship period that lasts up to six weeks. After they have chosen mates, they fall silent to avoid disrupting other penguins trying to find mates. They will resume using vocal calls after the female has laid an egg.

While the female is finding food, the male incubates the egg in a fold of skin called a brood pouch. After the chick hatches, the male feeds it with a nutrient-rich substance produced in its esophagus until the female returns. The female then takes over care while the male leaves to feed. At five months of age, the penguin chick is able to live independently. The dangers of starvation, predation by seals and seabirds, and harsh weather mean that only approximately 20 percent of chicks survive their first year of life.[21]

EMPEROR PENGUIN
Aptenodytes forsteri

SIZE
Wingspan of 2.5–2.9 feet (76–89 cm)

WEIGHT
55–99 pounds (25–45 kg)

RANGE
Antarctica

HABITAT
Coastlines and open sea

DIET
Fish, mollusks, crustaceans such as crabs

LIFE SPAN
15–20 years in the wild; 20–34 years in captivity

GOLDEN EAGLE

In addition to foxes, golden eagles hunt small mammals such as rabbits and squirrels, as well as larger prey such as coyotes.

A pair of golden eagles soars above the Canadian tundra. It has been days since they've eaten, and they're getting hungry. The eagles' eyes are trained on the open landscape below, searching for their next meal. They spot a fox, and their hunt begins.

The eagles are large, powerful birds, but the fox is still formidable prey. The pair works together to earn this meal. One eagle dives down while making loud noises, distracting the fox. The other loiters high above. When the fox turns toward the diving eagle, the second bird swoops down and strikes the fox's shoulders, knocking the mammal over.

The fox gets up to run away, but the persistent eagles repeat their attack. On the third try, the eagle digs into the fox with its sharp talons and hangs on. The fox is immobilized. The second eagle joins, and they finish off the fox. It's been another successful hunt for these effective predators.

BIRDS OF PREY

The golden eagle is one of the largest birds of prey in the world. It has mostly dark-brown feathers. There are faint gray bars on its tail, and golden feathers on the head and neck give the bird its name. Broad wings allow it to soar on warm updrafts called thermals.

The golden eagle is found in western North America, in northern Africa, and across much of Europe and Asia. It generally prefers areas that are completely or partly open, such as tundra, grasslands, and some forests. The eagle often lives in mountainous or hilly places with varied elevations. This kind of topography helps generate the thermals it uses for soaring.

The eagle eats mainly small mammals, such as rabbits, squirrels, and prairie dogs. It will sometimes eat birds

FUN FACT

Golden eagle fossils have been found in prehistoric settlements in the American Southwest, southern France, and northeastern Italy.

or reptiles too. More rarely it will seek out larger prey, including seals, foxes, or coyotes. Golden eagles usually hunt alone, but sometimes they work together in pairs.

NESTS AND YOUNG

Golden eagles commonly construct their nests in natural spots, such as cliffs or trees. However, they sometimes use human structures, building nests in windmills or electrical towers. Wherever the nests are located, they are built from sticks and lined with soft plant material, including leaves and mosses. The nests can be enormous. The largest nest ever observed was 8.5 feet (2.6 m) wide and an amazing 20 feet (6.1 m) tall.[22]

The eagles are monogamous, with pairs staying together for multiple years. During the courtship process they may chase each other through the sky, diving and soaring together. The female lays between one and four eggs each year, typically a few days apart. If there are multiple eggs, the first to hatch may kill its smaller, weaker siblings.

The young birds are able to fly at approximately ten weeks old. One to three months after that, they are able

GOLDEN EAGLE

to live independently, and they leave the nest. A few years later, between the ages of four and seven years, they will be able to breed. The eagles will find mates and establish their own nests.

A golden eagle takes flight from a snow-covered rock.

GOLDEN EAGLE
Aquila chrysaetos

SIZE
Wingspan of 6.1–7.2 feet (1.9–2.2 m)

WEIGHT
6.6–13.5 pounds (3–6.1 kg)

RANGE
Europe, Africa, Asia, North America

HABITAT
Mountainous areas

DIET
Mostly small mammals; sometimes seals, coyotes, badgers, foxes

LIFE SPAN
Up to 32 years in the wild; up to 46 years in captivity

GREAT BUSTARD

A male great bustard participates in a mating display.

The male great bustard strides across the rolling, grassy plain. The pattern of black and gold on his back, along with the grays and browns on his head and neck, make him blend in against the landscape. Nearby is a group of female great bustards. It is breeding season, and the male will try his best to impress them.

Suddenly the bustard's drab colors turn to a bright white, and the bird seems to increase in size. He has twisted his wings and tail around, ruffling out the bright white feathers on their undersides. He has also inflated a large pouch along his throat, making him appear larger. The bustard stamps his feet in place. It makes for a striking scene.

A female bustard approaches the male and circles him. The female has already visited and circled a few other males making their displays. She is selective. Only a small portion of the males will have the opportunity to mate.

GREAT BUSTARD BASICS

During the breeding season, the male great bustard has black and gold bars across his top. His head and neck are gray, with the lower neck darkening to brown. He has long, white barbs on his chin, looking somewhat like a beard or moustache. Outside of the breeding season, the male lacks these barbs, and his neck fades from brown to a pale gray. Female great bustards are colored similarly to the nonbreeding males, though they are much smaller.

The bustards live in places as far west as Spain and as far east as China, though they are not found everywhere in between, occupying

FUN FACT

Great bustards are among the heaviest birds capable of flight, with males weighing up to 40 pounds (18 kg).[23]

only selected spots across that range. The birds make their homes in flat, grassy habitats, as well as on agricultural fields. They may avoid farmlands if there is a heavy human presence nearby. Much of the birds' diet is made up of plants and invertebrates, though they sometimes feed on small mammals or amphibians too.

Great bustards often move slowly, though they can cover ground quickly if they need to. They lack opposable claws on their feet, meaning they are unable to perch in trees. When they are not flying, the birds are confined to the ground.

SOCIAL BIRDS

The great bustard is a highly social bird, living in groups called droves. Males and females have separate droves, with female droves visiting male ones during the breeding season. The mating process, featuring the male's striking display, is one of the bird's most notable behaviors. This system, in which groups of males compete for mates, is known as lekking. The female tends to pick the male with the most impressive display.

Once a male has mated, he has little involvement with the offspring. The female scrapes a nest into the ground and lays her eggs, typically two of them. She cares for the eggs, and after they hatch at approximately four weeks, she continues raising the young.

GREAT BUSTARD
Otis tarda

SIZE
Wingspan of 5.6–8.5 feet (1.7–2.6 m)

WEIGHT
7.3–40 pounds (3.3–18 kg)

RANGE
Spain, Germany, Eastern Europe, Russia, Kazakhstan, Middle East, Mongolia, China

HABITAT
Grassy plains, including farmlands

DIET
Plants, invertebrates, amphibians, small mammals, baby birds

LIFE SPAN
20–25 years in the wild

GREAT SPOTTED KIWI

Great spotted kiwis are nocturnal.

The sun has set on New Zealand's South Island. The great spotted kiwi, a gray, chicken-sized bird, emerges from its underground burrow. Now that it's night, it is time for the kiwi to find a meal.

The kiwi's eyesight is poor, but that doesn't matter much in the dark. It walks slowly, tapping the ground with its long, narrow bill. The sensitive bill, with the bird's nostrils near its tip, can detect the slight vibrations or changes in pressure that reveal the presence of prey hidden nearby.

The bird notices rustling in a pile of rotting leaves. It plunges its bill into the debris, snatching the earthworm within. The kiwi returns to its burrow before sunrise, where it will wait until nightfall before again venturing out to feed.

MAMMAL-LIKE BIRD

The great spotted kiwi is a flightless bird with a round body and short, thick legs. It has tiny, vestigial wings and no tail. The bird is covered in brownish-gray feathers patterned with white spots or bands. Its long bill is pale white in color. The kiwi's feathers are softer than those of flying birds, feeling almost like the fur of a mammal.

The kiwi has other similarities to mammals too. Because it doesn't need to fly, it has thicker skin and heavier bones than most other birds. Its body temperature is approximately 100 degrees Fahrenheit (38°C), relatively cool for a bird but more in line with the body temperatures of mammals.[24]

The great spotted kiwi is extremely limited geographically. It lives only in three distinct natural populations on the northwestern portion of New Zealand's South Island.[25] Other species of kiwis are also present on New Zealand's major and minor islands.

FUN FACT

The people of New Zealand have taken on the kiwi as a national symbol of their country. People from New Zealand are sometimes even called Kiwis.

BREEDING

Female great spotted kiwis lay just one egg per year. The egg, about 15 percent of the mother's body size, is one of the largest in proportion to body size of all birds.[26] The male and female take turns incubating the egg, with the female taking over in the night so the male can leave the nest to hunt for food. When a male begins incubating an egg, he loses some of the feathers on his underside. The direct skin-to-egg contact improves heat transfer.

With a single egg each year, kiwis put a great deal of effort into raising a small number of offspring. In ecology terms, they are K-strategists, relying on quality of care over quantity of offspring. The reverse are r-strategists. These animals produce a large number of offspring, many of which may die before reproducing themselves, in an effort to continue the species.

There are five known kiwi species, and all of them live in specific areas of New Zealand. Two of the species are endangered, and all five face at least some level of threat. Conservationists are working to ensure that kiwis do not go extinct.

KIWI DANGERS

Isolated in New Zealand, far from major landmasses, kiwis did not evolve alongside mammalian predators. They lack adaptations and instincts to defend against such threats. When human settlers introduced dogs and cats to New Zealand, these animals killed high proportions of young kiwis.

In the early 1900s, the government of New Zealand began taking steps to protect the birds. The birds still face threats. But modern conservation programs have helped improve the situation. Some protect kiwis from predators; other programs protect eggs or young kiwis to improve survival rates.

GREAT SPOTTED KIWI
Apteryx haastii

SIZE
1.4–1.8 feet (44–55 cm) long

WEIGHT
5.3–7.3 pounds (2.4–3.3 kg)

RANGE
New Zealand

HABITAT
Forested areas

DIET
Earthworms, insects, fruits

LIFE SPAN
20 years in the wild; up to 33 years in captivity

GREATER FLAMINGO

Young greater flamingos do not yet have the familiar pinkish color.

A series of croaking, goose-like cackles fills the air above the shallow Indian lagoon. There are thousands of greater flamingos here, their long legs allowing them to wade easily through the salty water. Some dip their heads below the surface to feed. But the greatest concentration of flamingos is on a small, muddy island that rises from the water.

On the island, a group of adult flamingos mills around, their trademark pale-pink color making them highly visible. They surround and supervise a cluster of smaller, younger, grayer flamingos. Some of the adults have offspring among the juvenile birds. Others do not. Predators do not go after adult flamingos, but lone juveniles can be vulnerable to attacks by larger birds. Staying together in these groups keeps the young safe.

APPEARANCE AND DISTRIBUTION

The greater flamingo has a pinkish-white body. It stands atop tall, skinny legs, and it has a long neck that is often held upright in an S shape. The bill is curved, with pink-and-black coloring. Greater flamingos are much paler in color than American flamingos, which have a more vivid reddish-pink hue.

Greater flamingos are found along the western, southern, and eastern coasts of Africa, as well as on Madagascar. They also

FUN FACT

While filter feeding, greater flamingos also take in tiny life-forms in the mud. Algae they consume are what provide the birds' pink coloring.

appear along shorelines in the Middle East and India. Smaller numbers occur in South America and in Europe. The birds require shallow water to feed, making their homes in salty lagoons, inland lakes, and muddy beaches.

The unique structure of the bird's bill allows the greater flamingo to filter water for food and pump out the excess water and mud. To feed, it dunks its head upside down in the water, reaching down into the mud for crustaceans, mollusks, insects, seeds, and decayed leaves. If the water level changes, leaving the flamingos unable to feed in this way, the group will travel to a new area that is more suitable.

NESTING AND YOUNG

Following a complex series of group mating displays, greater flamingos form pairs. Each pair builds a nest, usually from mud formed into a mound. The female generally lays a single egg, which is incubated in a divot in the center of the nest. The egg hatches in approximately 27 to 31 days.

As the young bird grows, it eventually moves into an area with other juveniles under the watch of adults. This is known as a crèche, a term that comes from the French word for "nursery." Forming a crèche is common among several kinds of birds.

Some of the adults are related to juveniles in the crèche, but some are not. It may seem unusual that birds would watch over offspring that are not their own. But scientists believe there may be an evolutionary explanation. The young raised in a crèche are more likely to survive than those that are not. This makes them more likely to pass along the crèche-forming behavior to their own offspring. Over the generations, raising young flamingos in a crèche becomes more common.

GREATER FLAMINGO
Phoenicopterus roseus

SIZE
Wingspan of 4.6–5.6 feet (1.4–1.7 m)

WEIGHT
4.2–6.6 pounds (1.9–3 kg)

RANGE
Mostly coastal areas in Africa, Europe, Asia, South America

HABITAT
Shallow waters, often salty

DIET
Crustaceans, mollusks, insects

LIFE SPAN
20–30 years on average in captivity and the wild

HOATZIN

Baby hoatzins are adept at climbing, thanks in part to their wing claws.

The dark-gray, week-old hoatzin sits peacefully in its nest. The ambient noises of the Amazon rain forest drift through the air, and a stream flows lazily just a few feet underneath the resting bird. Suddenly, a rustling sound nearby catches the bird's attention. It may be a predator. The hoatzin doesn't wait around to see what made the sound. The bird hurls itself out of the nest, splashing into the water below.

The hoatzin swims to safety, emerging from the water when the potential danger has passed. Now it needs to return to its nest in the tree, but it cannot yet fly. The dripping-wet bird walks over to the base of the tree and extends its wings. Claws on the ends of the wings grip the tree, and the hoatzin begins climbing wing over wing, bracing itself with its large feet. Before long it is safely back in the nest.

APPEARANCE AND LOCATION

Young hoatzins are mostly gray or black, but as they grow, they gain more colors. The adult has brownish feathers and a green tail with a white band on the end. The bare skin on its face is blue, and it has red eyes. A crest of reddish-brown feathers extends up from the head.

Hoatzins are found only in northern and central South America, in the Amazon rain forest. They nest in trees that overhang water in swamps, in marshes, or along the edges of lakes, rivers, or streams. Hoatzins can fly, but not well. They spend most of their time in the trees.

The birds are territorial. Once a pair establishes a nest, the two will defend the area using loud noises and aggressive postures. Young hoatzins generally live with their parents for a few years. As they grow and mature, they help with raising new offspring and defending the nest.

UNIQUE FEATURES

The hoatzin's wing claws are among its unique features. They are found only on young hoatzins, disappearing by the time they reach adulthood. These claws allow them to climb trees, which is especially useful after they dive from their nests to escape predators such

FUN FACT

The hoatzin's unusual digestion means that it sometimes gives off a smell that people have compared to animal manure. This has led to the nickname "the stink bird."

as monkeys, hawks, or snakes. It takes approximately 65 days for young hoatzins to develop the ability to fly, but they are skilled swimmers within five or six days of hatching.[27]

The configuration of the wing claws matches what is seen in fossils of dinosaurs, including the ancient bird *Archaeopteryx*. Many kinds of modern birds have such claws while they are developing before hatching. But the hoatzin retains the claws as a juvenile. Scientists have studied hoatzin wing claws to understand how flight evolved in birds.

Another feature that sets the hoatzin apart from other birds is its diet and its method of digesting food. It is the only bird that eats leaves as the main part of its diet. To do this, it has a greatly enlarged crop, a pouch in the throat that many kinds of birds use to store food. Inside the crop are bacteria that help break down the leaves that the hoatzin eats. Young birds do not have these bacteria. Adults regurgitate a sticky substance rich with the bacteria for the young to eat.

HOATZIN
Opisthocomus hoazin

SIZE
1.9–2.3 feet (59–70 cm) long

WEIGHT
1.5–2 pounds (0.7–0.9 kg)

RANGE
Northern and central South America

HABITAT
Swamps, marshes; edges of lakes, rivers, streams

DIET
Leaves, flowers, fruits

LIFE SPAN
Estimated 13 years in the wild

HOUSE SPARROW

House sparrows were introduced to North America to control pests, but as their numbers grew, they became pests themselves.

The New York City of 1851 looked vastly different from the city of today. There were no skyscrapers. The tallest structures were the church steeples that poked up between rows of buildings a handful of stories tall. Ships large and small filled the waterways around Manhattan Island, and Central Park was still an unrealized dream. It was into this landscape that a man named Nicholas Pike introduced 50 house sparrows to North America.[28]

The birds, among the first of their kind on the continent, were released in an attempt to control the linden moth. This insect was ruining the fruit trees and elms of Manhattan, and the sparrows were brought over from the United Kingdom to eat the pest. This plan succeeded, but it had unforeseen consequences. The population of house sparrows in North America exploded, and they became an invasive species, pushing out native birds and creating a nuisance for people. The birds meant to control pests had become pests themselves.

APPEARANCE AND HABITAT

The house sparrow has stouter legs and a thicker bill than sparrows native to North America. The bird has a brown back streaked with black, and its underside is a paler yellowish-brown. Male sparrows are distinguished from females by their white cheeks and the black feathers on their throats.

House sparrows are native to Europe, Asia, and North Africa. Humans have introduced them to other regions, and now they live everywhere but the poles. The birds' existence is deeply linked to humans. Their habitats are areas with a human presence, including city neighborhoods, suburban zones, and agricultural lands. In fact, house sparrows are typically not present in places that don't have people. They eat insects, seeds from the ground, and human-provided birdseed, depending on what's available.

FUN FACT

Less than a century after the introduction of 50 birds in New York, the population of house sparrows in North America was estimated at 150 million.[29]

HOUSE SPARROW

Many types of predators threaten the house sparrow, including owls, raccoons, snakes, and domestic dogs and cats. When searching the ground for food, the birds will form groups so that more of them are alert to possible threats. This improves their chances of survival.

PROTECTING THE NEST

House sparrows build their nests in natural spots such as trees or in human-made structures such as crevices inside or around buildings. A male and female pair up for each breeding season. The female lays one to eight eggs at a time, and she does this up to four times during a breeding season, which lasts from February through August in North America. The male and female share responsibility for incubating the eggs, which hatch in approximately two weeks.

The birds fiercely defend the nest and the surrounding area. They threaten or even attack other species of birds that encroach on their territory. Male sparrows defend against male invaders, and females defend against female invaders.

In places where they are invasive, the house sparrow's nesting habits have created problems for native species. In North America, birds such as bluebirds, chickadees, and woodpeckers are affected. Sparrows will take over their nesting spots, physically removing both adult and juvenile birds from the nests.

HOUSE SPARROW
Passer domesticus

SIZE
5.9–6.7 inches (15–17 cm) long

WEIGHT
0.89 ounces (25.3 g) on average

RANGE
Native to Europe, Asia, North Africa; invasive worldwide except at the poles

HABITAT
Near human presence in urban, residential, agricultural areas

DIET
Seeds, insects

LIFE SPAN
13 years maximum in the wild

MALLARD

Male mallards are more brilliantly colored than females.

On a crisp Midwestern autumn day, a familiar rasping birdcall rises through the tall grasses of the marshy wetlands. Multiple notes ring out in sequence. The first few are the loudest and longest; they decrease steadily in volume and duration as they continue. The call seems to be contagious—suddenly similar calls begin to echo across the landscape. The unmistakable quacking of the mallard duck fills the air. Human hunters hide nearby, their shotguns at the ready.

A FAMOUS BIRD

The mallard is the most widespread duck in North America, and it is among the most easily recognizable ducks in the world.[30] The male has a brown breast, a brownish-gray topside, and a gray underside. His head is a dark iridescent green, and a narrow ring of white encircles his neck. Iridescent blue feathers are visible at the rear of his wings when the wings are outstretched. The female shares this blue feather coloring, but otherwise she is drabber in color, with brown feathers all over the rest of her body.

Mallards are common in North America, and they are also found in Europe, Asia, Africa, and South America. Excellent swimmers and divers, they prefer to live in wetlands with shallow water. Either fresh water or salt water is suitable, as long as the water is not fast flowing and there is enough vegetation to provide some cover.

The mallard is a filter feeder. Water enters its bill near the tip and exits near the sides, passing through closely spaced structures called lamellae that trap food and allow water to leave. Mallards mainly eat small invertebrates such as dragonflies, snails, and earthworms, but they will also eat some aquatic vegetation and grains from farmers' fields.

QUACKING

With their distinctive coloring, male mallards are easily distinguishable on sight. The females' coloring is duller, but they are just as distinguishable by sound. Only the females make the famous "quack" call. This call, known to experts as the decrescendo call, is made up of two to ten notes that decrease in volume.

Ducks use the call to declare their location to other ducks and to beckon others to join them. They may use it to get the attention of separated mates or ducklings. Because of this function, some experts also refer to it as the hail call. When one female in a flock begins quacking, others typically make the call too.

HUNTING

Mallards are among the most popular game birds, with large numbers hunted in the United States and Canada. In the 2010s, approximately 3.5 million mallards were hunted per year

FUN FACT

Mallards mate with other duck species across their vast range, producing hybrid offspring.

in the United States.[31] Still, the overall population is stable. Hunters pay license fees to hunt mallards, and that money helps fund habitat protection and management of the species.

Hunters can use duck calls to their advantage. A large industry exists around devices designed to simulate calls and attract nearby ducks. Hunters blow into these devices to make the sounds. Among the calls they use is the famous hail call. Mastering this technique to make realistic calls with the proper timing and sound can be a complicated task.

Decoys and duck calls are common duck-hunting equipment.

MALLARD
Anas platyrhynchos

SIZE
Wingspan of 2.5–3.3 feet (0.75–1 m)

WEIGHT
2.2 pounds (1 kg) on average

RANGE
North America, Asia, Europe, Africa, South America

HABITAT
Wetlands

DIET
Insects, vegetation

LIFE SPAN
5–10 years in the wild; up to 10 years in captivity

RED-BILLED TROPICBIRD

Red-billed tropicbirds spend most of their time over the open sea.

It's a sunny day in the Caribbean. The waves roll gently to the horizon, and there is no land in sight. Without warning a small, silver shape begins to emerge at a high speed from the water's surface. The fish stretches out its large fins and gives one last push from its tail before leaving the water completely.

The flying fish begins a glide that may go for hundreds of feet. It has escaped successfully from an underwater predator. But it was not counting on a predator from above. A red-billed tropicbird swoops down and snatches the flying fish in midair. Its beak's jagged edges hold the squirming fish firmly in place. It will make a filling meal for the tropicbird's hungry chick, waiting back in its island nest.

BIRD OF THE TROPICS

The red-billed tropicbird is covered mostly in white feathers, except for areas of black feathers behind the eyes and along the leading edges of its wings. Its bill—bright red when the bird reaches adulthood—gives this species of tropicbird its name. Males and females look similar, except the males are somewhat larger.

FUN FACT

The feet of red-billed tropicbirds are set too far back on their bodies to walk effectively. When moving on land, they glide on their stomachs.

Red-billed tropicbirds often build nests in rocky crevices.

RED-BILLED TROPICBIRD

Red-billed tropicbirds live in the warm regions in and near Earth's tropics. They are found in the Pacific, Atlantic, and Indian Oceans, as well as in the Caribbean Sea. The birds are pelagic, meaning they mostly live over the open sea. They land on remote islands, such as the Galápagos Islands off the coast of South America, to breed.

The bird's diet is made up of small fish, most commonly flying fish, and sometimes squid. Excellent swimmers, red-billed tropicbirds usually hunt by hovering in midair above

the water before plunging in to grab prey. Scientists have also observed them catching flying fish during the fish's brief glides. When flying, red-billed tropicbirds must beat their wings at a fast pace to remain in the air over the open sea.

BREEDING AND NESTING

Red-billed tropicbirds perform complex aerobatics during courtship displays, flying backward and in circles. Once a bird finds a mate, the two establish an island nest together. The nest is generally in a rocky crevice or a scraped-away portion of softer ground. The male often constructs it using his bill and feet. The female lays a single egg, which is incubated for approximately 42 days. The parents take turns incubating in shifts.

RED-BILLED TROPICBIRD
Phaethon aethereus

SIZE
Wingspan of 3.25–3.5 feet (0.99–1.07 m)

WEIGHT
1.5 pounds (0.7 kg)

RANGE
In and near the tropics

HABITAT
Open ocean; breeds on remote islands

DIET
Small fish, squid

LIFE SPAN
16 years in the wild

After the chick hatches, the cooperation between parents continues. They take turns feeding the young. To do this, they put their bills down the chick's throat and regurgitate food. By six weeks old, the chick has become adult sized. Six weeks later, it takes its first flight. When the bird leaves the nest, its bill is dark gray in color. As it ages, it will gain its trademark red bill.

ROCK PIGEON

Cher Ami was a rock pigeon who delivered important messages during World War I.

In October 1918, the end of World War I (1914–1918) was just a month away, but the fighting was still fierce. Above the cratered battlefields of France flew many domesticated rock pigeons, also known as carrier pigeons. Using their natural abilities to find their way back to their nests, these birds carried military messages on tiny capsules attached to their legs.

A dozen times, a bird named Cher Ami carried critical messages for the US Army as the American forces battled the Germans. The final mission of Cher Ami's career came on October 4. A group of US troops had become isolated from the main body of the army, and it was surrounded by the enemy. Cher Ami carried a message requesting a rescue. He was shot in mid-flight through the breast and leg, but he kept going and delivered the message. The 194 survivors of the so-called Lost Battalion were saved.

Cher Ami survived the war and returned to the United States, but he succumbed to his wounds on June 13, 1919.[32]

APPEARANCE AND RANGE

The rock pigeon is dark blue-gray across much of its body, including its head, chest, and back. A pair of dark bands stretches across the wings, and the tail has another dark band. One of the bird's most recognizable features is the iridescent coloring on its neck, in which hues of yellow, green, red, and purple are visible. The iridescence is less visible on females than on males.

Rock pigeons are native to Europe, North Africa, and southwestern Asia. They were introduced elsewhere by humans, including to North America by European colonists in the early 1600s. Today they are found worldwide.

In the wild, rock pigeons often live on seaside cliffs, near farm fields, or in areas with low shrub vegetation. They also make their homes in human settlements, including farm buildings in rural places and on skyscrapers in urban areas. The rock pigeon diet varies based on where the birds live.

Usually they eat seeds and fruits, though in cities they will also eat discarded human food, such as popcorn, cake, peanuts, and bread.

HOMING AND DOMESTICATION

The rock pigeon has an impressive ability to find its home after foraging for food in distant places. Scientists have extensively studied how the bird does this, but the details are not yet fully understood. They believe that the birds first determine what direction is home, then use a method to stay pointed in the right direction in flight.

It's not clear how rock pigeons figure out the direction. The leading hypotheses include using the senses of smell or hearing or perhaps sensing Earth's magnetic field. The way rock pigeons maintain the right direction is better understood. They use the location of the sun in the sky, and when the sun is obscured by clouds, they use Earth's magnetic field.

However this navigation skill works, humans have long recognized it, and they have domesticated rock pigeons to take advantage of it. Starting as long ago as the time of ancient

FUN FACT
During World War I, France had a fleet of some 30,000 messenger pigeons working for the military.[33]

ROCK PIGEON

Rome, people have used pigeons to carry messages to distant places. During World War I, Cher Ami was one of 600 birds used by the US Army Signal Corps.[34]

Advancing communication technology has replaced the need for message-carrying birds, but rock pigeons are still raised for sport. Pigeon racing has become a popular pastime. People raise the birds to return home as quickly as possible. A racing rock pigeon may travel 300 miles (480 km) in just seven hours—an average speed of more than 40 miles per hour (64 kmh).[35]

The sport of pigeon racing began in Belgium, and the world governing body for the sport is headquartered there.

ROCK PIGEON
Columba livia

SIZE
0.95–1.2 feet (29–36 cm) long

WEIGHT
12.7 ounces (359 g) on average

RANGE
Native to Europe, North Africa, southwestern Asia; introduced worldwide except at the poles

HABITAT
Seaside cliffs, agricultural areas, human settlements

DIET
Seeds, fruits; discarded human foods in urban areas

LIFE SPAN
6 years on average in the wild; up to 35 years in captivity

RUBY-THROATED HUMMINGBIRD

Ruby-throated hummingbirds are less than four inches (10 cm) long.

The ruby-throated hummingbird zooms southward. Below it, the Gulf coastline of the United States gives way to a seemingly endless stretch of water. The daylight hours in the American South have been getting shorter by the day, so it is time for the bird to migrate. As it leaves land behind, the hummingbird is embarking on a nonstop journey of some 500 miles (805 km) to its wintering grounds in Mexico. There, it will find enough food to breed and raise its young before returning home. This voyage will be no easy feat for a bird weighing not much more than a penny.

APPEARANCE AND FLIGHT

The ruby-throated hummingbird is iridescent green with a white underside. The males have the bright, metallic-red throat that gives the species its name. The female's throat is duller and grayer in color. Another characteristic distinguishing the sexes is the tail shape—the male's is forked, and the female's is square.

Like other hummingbirds, the ruby-throated hummingbird is capable of flying feats unlike those of most bird species. It flaps its wings at 53 beats per second, allowing it to hover in place and generating the distinctive humming noise of its flight.[36] The bird is also capable of flying backward and even upside down.

This flying skill is necessary to get the ruby-throated hummingbird's preferred food: nectar from red, tube-shaped flowers. It hovers in front of the flower, then it uses its long, thin beak to get at the nectar within. This also means the bird is an important

RUBY-THROATED HUMMINGBIRD

pollinator in the ecosystems where it lives. The bird must do a lot of feeding, as its flight takes a lot of energy to sustain. A ruby-throated hummingbird can eat twice its body weight in food every day.

FUN FACT

The ruby-throated hummingbird's heart beats at more than 1,200 beats per minute when flying.[37] A typical resting human heart rate is 60 to 100 beats per minute.[38]

MIGRATION

The birds live in the eastern areas of North and Central America, breeding in the United States and Canada and making long migratory journeys to Mexico and Central America for the winter. Some birds make the trip over land, looping around the Gulf of Mexico, but others fly directly across the water, completing the lengthy voyage in under a day.

For such small birds, making a long, nonstop flight requires preparation. The birds eat enough food to double their body weight before departing, providing fuel for the trek. The return to breeding grounds in the spring is timed so that the local plants are beginning to flower when the hummingbirds arrive, providing a plentiful food source.

In both its breeding grounds and its winter homes, the ruby-throated hummingbird lives in natural woodlands, gardens, and orchards. It is also found in clearings and in the edges of forests. The breeding grounds are the only places where ruby-throated hummingbirds come into contact with each other, doing so when they mate. The rest of the time they live solitary lives.

RUBY-THROATED HUMMINGBIRD
Archilochus colubris

SIZE
3–3.5 inches (7.5–9 cm) long

WEIGHT
0.12–0.13 ounces (3.4–3.8 g)

RANGE
North America and Central America

HABITAT
Woodlands, gardens, orchards

DIET
Nectar, insects

LIFE SPAN
5–9.1 years in the wild

SCARLET MACAW

The striking coloring of the scarlet macaw makes it a target of poaching.

In the Moskitia region of Honduras, men wearing jeans, baseball caps, and neon-yellow shirts patrol a forest. Some of them have rifles slung over their shoulders—a necessary precaution, because poachers have shot at the conservation team before. The men reach a tree. One of them gears up to climb it, and he ascends into the canopy. He is checking on the nest of a scarlet macaw.

Poachers have devastated the scarlet macaw population in this region. In 2014, every single nest in the conservation area was targeted. Poachers stole young macaws,

which are profitable in the international trade of illegal wildlife. But things have been changing. Supported by a 2017 grant from the US Fish and Wildlife Service, community conservation teams are patrolling the forest and protecting the macaws. Some of the patrol members were once poachers themselves. Now they earn a living defending these beautiful birds.

APPEARANCE

Scarlet macaws are among the most striking and colorful birds on Earth. Scarlet feathers cover their heads and shoulders. They have yellow feathers on their backs and in the middle of their wings. Their tails and wing tips are blue. On their faces, short white feathers surround yellow eyes. It is their vivid coloring that makes them so attractive to poachers.

The macaws are mostly found in the Amazon basin of South America, though populations also exist in Mexico and Central America. They live high in the trees of the rain

DIET

Scarlet macaws have sharp, powerful bills. This allows them to tear into fruits before they have ripened, as well as through nuts that other animals are unable to eat. Additionally, structures within the beak allow them to grind up and digest hard seeds. As a result of these adaptations, scarlet macaws have more feeding options than their competitors in the rain forest. The birds have been known to eat 126 separate species of plants.[39]

Scarlet macaws also eat nonfood items. Groups of the birds have been observed eating clay on riverbanks,

FUN FACT

A scarlet macaw generally uses its left foot to pick up food or grab things, using its right foot to support its body.

a practice known as geophagy. Scientists have found that this helps the birds digest harsh foods, such as unripe fruits and toxic fruits that other vertebrates can't eat.

PAIR BONDS

Scarlet macaws form pair bonds that last for life. Once a macaw has found a mate, the two are rarely seen alone. They fly and nest together. Mates will show affection for one another by licking one another's face and preening, or cleaning one another's feathers.

The female macaw lays two to four eggs, which she incubates for approximately 24 or 25 days. She does most of the incubation. After the eggs hatch, the male feeds the young macaws by regurgitating food into their mouths. The pair does not have any more eggs until the existing young are able to live independently, a process that can take one or two years.

SCARLET MACAW
Ara macao

SIZE
2.9 feet (89 cm) long on average, including the tail

WEIGHT
2.2 pounds (1 kg) on average

RANGE
Southern Mexico, Central America, the Amazon basin

HABITAT
Rain forests

DIET
Fruits, nuts

LIFE SPAN
40–50 years in the wild; up to 75 years in captivity

WANDERING ALBATROSS

The wandering albatross spends most of its life out at sea.

Held aloft on its massive wings, which stretch 11.5 feet (3.5 m) from tip to tip, the wandering albatross surveys the vast blue sea below.[40] It has spotted a fishing boat miles in the distance. These vessels are popular places for albatrosses to feed. The fishing boats are filled with defenseless prey for birds who are able to find them at sea.

The majestic seabird has no idea that the boat's crew is fishing illegally in this area. But scientists monitoring the situation from far away do. Weeks ago, the scientists attached a lightweight device to the albatross's back at its island breeding site. The device senses the radar signals emitted by boats, detects the location using GPS, and transmits data back to the scientists. The wandering albatross is helping to map the movements of illegal fishing vessels. And it gets a hearty meal of fish in the process.

APPEARANCE AND HABITAT

The wandering albatross has the largest wingspan of any bird.[41] The feathers on its body range from white to brown, and its wings are partly or mostly black. Its bill is pink. Male wandering albatrosses are somewhat larger than females.

The albatrosses are found in the Southern Hemisphere. They nest and breed on subantarctic islands, but they are mostly pelagic the rest of the time, meaning they spend long stretches of time at sea. The birds eat fish, squid, and sometimes crustaceans. They typically grab prey on the surface, though people have also observed them using shallow dives to hunt.

WANDERING ALBATROSS

Wandering albatrosses search for food in small groups. They commonly follow fishing boats, aware of the feeding opportunities they provide. However, there can be danger in this. The birds can become snagged in the fishing equipment and get hurt or killed.

BREEDING AND YOUNG

Wandering albatrosses form pair bonds that last for life. After months spent feeding at sea,

FUN FACT

A wandering albatross can circumnavigate the planet in just 46 days, keeping up a speed of approximately 81 miles per hour (130 kmh) for eight hours at a time.[42]

98

male albatrosses arrive at the same island breeding sites they used in previous years. All the males arrive within the span of a few days. They search for previously used nests, reusing them if possible and constructing new ones if necessary. The female birds arrive later, joining their mates.

Females lay one egg per year. If it does not survive to hatching, the pair will wait until the next year to try again. If it does survive, it will hatch in approximately 78 days. The parents take turns incubating the egg, and after it hatches they take turns gathering food. Chicks are unable to feed themselves for approximately the first nine months of life, so they rely completely on their parents. By around ten months, they are able to fly, and they become independent at this time.

Young, independent albatrosses may travel vast distances when they go out to sea on their own. One study analyzed the travel of juvenile birds in the first year after leaving the nest. It found that they traveled an average of 114,000 miles (184,000 km) in that year, circling the globe multiple times.[43]

WANDERING ALBATROSS
Diomedea exulans

SIZE
Wingspan of up to 11.5 feet (3.5 m)

WEIGHT
17.9 pounds (8.1 kg) on average

RANGE
Southern Hemisphere

HABITAT
Open ocean; breeds on subantarctic islands

DIET
Fish, squid, crustaceans

LIFE SPAN
60 years maximum in the wild

ESSENTIAL FACTS

BIRD FEATURES

- All birds have feathers, have four-chambered hearts, and lay hard-shell eggs.

- Many, but not all, birds are capable of flight. Some that are not able to fly are adept at moving on land and in the water.

- Many birds have excellent vision, helping them hunt and navigate in flight.

- Birds use a wide variety of vocalizations to communicate.

NOTABLE SPECIES

- The chicken (*Gallus gallus domesticus*), domesticated long ago, has become a vitally important bird to humans. Used for eggs and meat, it is one of the most widely farmed animals in the world.

- The common ostrich (*Struthio camelus*) is the world's largest bird by weight, demonstrating how big birds can become when they lose the need and ability to fly.

- The mallard (*Anas platyrhynchos*) is widely recognizable both by sight and by sound; males have a distinctive green head, and females make the famous hail call.

- The wandering albatross (*Diomedea exulans*) has the largest wingspan of any bird on Earth, stretching as wide as 11.5 feet (3.5 m) from wing tip to wing tip.

BIRDS' ROLES ON EARTH

Birds live in nearly every habitat on Earth, including the arid deserts of Africa, the lush Amazon rain forest, the bustling cityscape of New York City, and the frigid shores of Antarctica. As both predator and prey, they play a role in food chains across the globe. Some species, such as house sparrows (*Passer domesticus*), have become invasive after being introduced to new areas by humans. Ruby-throated hummingbirds (*Archilochus colubris*) help out their ecosystems by serving as pollinators.

BIRDS AND CONSERVATION

Bird species are threatened by human encroachment, habitat destruction, and pollution. The great spotted kiwi (*Apteryx haastii*) faced predation from animals that people brought to its island home. Poachers target scarlet macaws (*Ara macao*) for sale in the illegal wildlife trade. People and governments are recognizing the threats that birds face, and they have launched programs to mitigate these problems and save threatened species.

BIRDS AROUND THE WORLD

102

GLOSSARY

adaptation
A change in traits within a population that allows an individual or species to be more successful in its environment.

aerobatics
Impressive midair maneuvers.

carrion
The flesh of dead animals.

domesticate
To adapt to live among or be of use to people.

ecology
The study of living things and their environments.

incubate
To keep eggs warm until they are ready to hatch.

invasive
Describing an organism that arrives in a new ecosystem, takes over, and causes harm.

invertebrate
An animal without a spinal column.

iridescent
Having the appearance of changing color as the viewing angle changes, such as on a soap bubble.

omnivorous
Describing an organism that eats both animal and plant matter.

poacher

A person who illegally hunts or captures an animal.

pollinator

An organism that transfers pollen from one plant to another, facilitating the receiving plant's reproduction.

poultry

Domesticated fowl, such as chickens and turkeys, raised for meat and eggs.

regurgitate

To bring swallowed food back up through the throat, often to feed young.

ruff

Prominent feathers on or around a bird's face or neck.

succulent

A plant that stores water in its leaves, thriving in dry climates.

talon

A claw on a bird's foot.

vertebrate

An animal with a spinal column and a brain that is part of its nervous system.

vestigial

Remaining in a form that is not able to function because it is small or not fully developed.

ADDITIONAL RESOURCES

SELECTED BIBLIOGRAPHY

Alderton, David. *The Complete Illustrated Encyclopedia of Birds of the World*. Lorenz, 2012.

"Animal Diversity Web." *University of Michigan Museum of Zoology*, 2020, animaldiversity.org. Accessed 7 Dec. 2020.

"Birds of the World." *Cornell Lab of Ornithology*, 2020, birdsoftheworld.org. Accessed 7 Dec. 2020.

FURTHER READINGS

Alderfer, Jonathan and Noah Strycker. *National Geographic Backyard Guide to the Birds of North America*. National Geographic, 2019.

Hand, Carol. *The Evolution of Birds*. Abdo, 2019.

Sibley, David Allen. *What It's Like to Be a Bird*. Knopf, 2020.

ONLINE RESOURCES

To learn more about birds, please visit **abdobooklinks.com** or scan this QR code. These links are routinely monitored and updated to provide the most current information available.

MORE INFORMATION

For more information on this subject, contact or visit the following organizations:

James Newman Clark Bird Museum

Phillips Science Hall 330
101 Roosevelt Ave.
Eau Claire, WI 54701
715-836-4166
uwec.edu/academics/college-arts-sciences/departments-programs/biology/explore-opportunities/academic-facilities/james-newman-clark-bird-museum/

The James Newman Clark Bird Museum, located at the University of Wisconsin-Eau Claire, features dioramas showing birds in their natural habitats. Admission is free to the public.

Smithsonian National Museum of Natural History

Tenth St. & Constitution Ave. NW
Washington, DC 20560
naturalexperience@si.edu
naturalhistory.si.edu

The Smithsonian National Museum of Natural History's Division of Birds has a vast collection of more than 640,000 specimens representing approximately 85 percent of known bird species.

SOURCE NOTES

1. Mindy Weisberger. "Are Birds Dinosaurs?" *LiveScience*, 20 Jan. 2020, livescience.com. Accessed 1 Feb. 2021.

2. Frank Gill. "Bird." *Britannica*, 30 Oct. 2020, britannica.com. Accessed 1 Feb. 2021.

3. Gareth Huw Davies. "Parenthood." *PBS: The Life of Birds by David Attenborough*, n.d., pbs.org/lifeofbirds. Accessed 1 Feb. 2021.

4. "Eagle Eyes." *National Eagle Center*, n.d., nationaleaglecenter.org. Accessed 1 Feb. 2021.

5. Gill, "Bird."

6. Gill, "Bird."

7. Walter D. Koenig et al. "Acorn Woodpecker." *Birds of the World*, 4 Mar. 2020, birdsoftheworld.org. Accessed 1 Feb. 2021.

8. Koenig et al., "Acorn Woodpecker."

9. "Greater Rhea." *National Geographic*, n.d., nationalgeographic.com. Accessed 1 Feb. 2021.

10. "Puffin FAQs." *Audubon Project Puffin*, n.d., projectpuffin.audubon.org. Accessed 1 Feb. 2021.

11. Peter E. Lowther et al. "Atlantic Puffin." *Birds of the World*, 4 Mar. 2020, birdsoftheworld.org. Accessed 1 Feb. 2021.

12. Elizabeth Poole. "Pelecanus Conspicillatus." *Animal Diversity Web*, 2011, animaldiversity.org. Accessed 1 Feb. 2021.

13. Poole, "Pelecanus Conspicillatus."

14. Carl D. Marti et al. "Barn Owl." *Birds of the World*, 4 Mar. 2020, birdsoftheworld.org. Accessed 1 Feb. 2021.

15. Ed. Robert Lewis. "Chicken." *Britannica*, 20 June 2016, britannica.com. Accessed 1 Feb. 2021.

16. "Broiler Chicken Industry Key Facts 2019." *National Chicken Council*, n.d., nationalchickencouncil.org. Accessed 1 Feb. 2021.

17. George W. Archibald et al. "Common Crane." *Birds of the World*, 4 Mar. 2020, birdsoftheworld.org. Accessed 1 Feb. 2021.

18. Gill, "Bird."

19. Bob Sundstrom. "Which Bird Is the Fastest Runner?" *Audubon*, Sept. 2017, audubon.org. Accessed 1 Feb. 2021.

20. Isabel Martínez et al. "Emperor Penguin." *Birds of the World*, 4 Mar. 2020, birdsoftheworld.org. Accessed 1 Feb. 2021.

21. Sarah Wilber. "Aptenodytes Forsteri." *Animal Diversity Web*, 2020, animaldiversity.org. Accessed 1 Feb. 2021.

22. Kari Kirschbaum and Alicia Ivory. "Aquila Chrysaetos." *Animal Diversity Web*, 2002, animaldiversity.org. Accessed 1 Feb. 2021.

23. Nigel Collar and Ernest Garcia. "Great Bustard." *Birds of the World*, 4 Mar. 2020, birdsoftheworld.org. Accessed 1 Feb. 2021.

24. "Kiwi." *San Diego Zoo*, n.d., animals.sandiegozoo.com. Accessed 1 Feb. 2021.

25. H. A. Robertson. "Great Spotted Kiwi." *New Zealand Birds Online*, 2017, nzbirdsonline.org.nz. Accessed 1 Feb. 2021.

26. Alina Bradford. "Facts about Kiwis." *LiveScience*, 9 Feb. 2017, livescience.com. Accessed 1 Feb. 2021.

27. Shawn M. Billerman. "Hoatzin." *Birds of the World*, 4 Mar. 2020, birdsoftheworld.org. Accessed 1 Feb. 2021.

28. Emily Wang and Jared Gerber. "Mae Grant Playground: House Sparrows in New York City Parks." *NYC Parks*, n.d., nycgovparks.org. Accessed 1 Feb. 2021.

29. Peter E. Lowther and Calvin L. Cink. "House Sparrow." *Birds of the World*, 4 Mar. 2020, birdsoftheworld.org. Accessed 1 Feb. 2021.

30. Nancy Drilling et al. "Mallard." *Birds of the World*, 4 Mar. 2020, birdsoftheworld.org. Accessed 1 Feb. 2021.

31. Drilling et al., "Mallard."

32. "Cher Ami." *Smithsonian*, n.d., si.edu. Accessed 1 Feb. 2021.

33. Mary Blume. "The Hallowed History of the Carrier Pigeon." *New York Times*, 30 Jan. 2004, nytimes.com. Accessed 1 Feb. 2021.

34. Blume, "The Hallowed History of the Carrier Pigeon."

35. Peter E. Lowther and Richard F. Johnston. "Rock Pigeon." *Birds of the World*, 4 Mar. 2020, birdsoftheworld.org. Accessed 1 Feb. 2021.

36. Kari Kirschbaum et al. "Archilochus Colubris." *Animal Diversity Web*, 2000, animaldiversity.org. Accessed 1 Feb. 2021.

37. "Hummingbirds." *Smithsonian's National Zoo & Conservation Biology Institute*, n.d., nationalzoo.si.edu. Accessed 1 Feb. 2021.

38. Edward R. Laskowski. "What's a Normal Resting Heart Rate?" *Mayo Clinic*, 2 Oct. 2020, mayoclinic.org. Accessed 1 Feb. 2021.

39. Nigel Collar et al. "Scarlet Macaw." *Birds of the World*, 4 Mar. 2020, birdsoftheworld.org. Accessed 1 Feb. 2021.

40. Gill, "Bird."

41. Lauren Scopel. "Diomedea Exulans." *Animal Diversity Web*, 2007, animaldiversity.org. Accessed 1 Feb. 2021.

42. Josep del Hoyo et al. "Wandering Albatross." *Birds of the World*, 4 Mar. 2020, birdsoftheworld.org. Accessed 1 Feb. 2021.

43. Del Hoyo et al., "Wandering Albatross."

INDEX

acorns, 13–15
Africa, 17, 34, 37, 39, 41–42, 43, 46, 47, 53, 55, 65, 67, 73, 75, 77, 79, 85, 87
albatrosses, 8, 96–99
Amazon rain forest, 68–69, 93, 95
amphibians, 39, 58, 59
Antarctica, 29, 31, 49–50, 51
Archaeopteryx, 71
Asia, 34, 37, 39, 42, 43, 46, 53, 55, 67, 73, 75, 77, 79, 85, 87
Atlantic Ocean, 20–23, 82
Australia, 24, 27

beak shapes, 7, 17, 23, 39, 49, 80, 89, 94
birdsong, 9
bird-watching, 5
brood parasitism, 42–43
bustards, 56–59

Canada, 22, 23, 78, 91
cardinals, 8, 10
Caribbean Sea, 80, 82
carrier pigeons, 84–87

Central America, 14, 15, 91, 93, 95
Cher Ami, 84–85, 87
chickens, 8, 32–35
Clarke, Julia, 5
classification of birds, 10–11
condors, 16–19
conservation, 63, 92–93
cranes, 36–39
crèches, 67
cuckoos, 40–43

Darwin, Charles, 5
defense, 15, 39, 47, 63, 65, 68, 70, 74–75
diving birds, 9, 20–21, 23, 49, 68, 70–71, 77, 97
domestication, 4, 33–34, 84, 86–87
ducks, 7, 76–79

eagles, 7, 8, 52–55
eggs, 4, 33–34, 40–43
  number laid, 10, 22, 48, 54, 59, 62, 66, 75, 83, 95, 99

size, 7, 47, 62
strength, 7
Europe, 22, 23, 34, 37, 39, 42, 43, 53, 55, 59, 66, 67, 73, 75, 77, 79, 85, 87

farming, 32–35, 46
feathers, 6
filter feeding, 7, 65, 66, 77
fish, 20–21, 22, 23, 24, 26–27, 39, 49, 51, 80, 82–83, 96–98, 99
flamingos, 64–67
flightless birds, 8–9, 17, 45, 49, 61

Galápagos Islands, 5, 82
geophagy, 94–95
granaries, 12–15
Gulf of Mexico, 88, 91

hearts, 6, 90
herons, 37
hoatzins, 68–71

hummingbirds, 6, 7, 8, 11, 88–91
hunting by humans, 4–5, 46, 76, 78–79

incubation, 9–10, 39, 48–51, 59, 62, 66, 75, 83, 95, 99
Indian Ocean, 82
invasive species, 72–75
invertebrates, 7, 14, 15, 26, 33, 39, 41, 42, 43, 58, 59, 63, 66, 67, 73, 75, 77, 79, 91

keratin, 6
kiwis, 60–63

lekking, 59

macaws, 92–95
mammals, 6, 16, 18, 19, 31, 47, 52–54, 55, 58, 59, 61, 63
Manhattan, 72
mating displays, 9, 50, 56–57, 59, 66, 83
Mexico, 14, 15, 88, 91, 93, 95
migration, 39, 42–43, 88, 91

monogamy, 30, 50, 54, 95, 98
mythical birds, 4

nesting, 9–10, 31, 33, 39, 40–41, 47, 54–55, 59, 62, 66–67, 68–70, 75, 83, 92–95, 97, 99
New Zealand, 27, 60–63
North America, 53, 55, 72–73, 75, 76–77, 79, 85, 91

ostriches, 6, 7, 8, 9, 11, 44–47
owls, 28–31, 74

Pacific Ocean, 82
pelicans, 24–27
penguins, 9, 11, 21, 48–51
pigeons, 84–87
   racing, 87
Pike, Nicholas, 72
poaching, 92–93
puffins, 20–23

regurgitation, 49, 51, 71, 83, 95
relationship to humans, 4–5, 6, 22, 32–35, 46, 73, 76, 78–79, 84–87, 92–93, 96

reptiles, 15, 26, 27, 39, 54, 71, 74
rheas, 17
robins, 8

scavengers, 17–19
scientists, 5, 10, 12, 13, 23, 29–30, 33, 67, 71, 83, 86, 95, 96
South America, 16–17, 19, 66, 67, 69, 71, 77, 79, 82, 93
Southeast Asia, 34, 37, 42, 43
sparrows, 10–11, 72–75
swans, 8

thermals, 18, 53
tropicbirds, 80–83

United States, 14, 15, 34–35, 78–79, 85, 88, 91

vision, 8, 28, 31, 60

warblers, 40–41
wing claws, 68, 70–71
woodpeckers, 7, 11, 12–15, 75
World War I, 84–87

ABOUT THE AUTHOR
Arnold Ringstad

Arnold Ringstad has written more than 100 books for audiences ranging from elementary school to high school. He especially enjoys reading and writing about science, including ecology. He lives in Minnesota with his wife and their cat.

ABOUT THE CONSULTANT
Kevin R. Burgio, PhD

Kevin R. Burgio, PhD, is a research scientist at the University of Connecticut, where he studies parrot conservation, extinction, and the role climate change may play in reshaping ecosystems in the future. He also writes about parrots and is an advocate for diversity, equity, and inclusion in higher education. He spends his spare time with his daughter and two cats, usually fishing, hiking, rockhounding, or reading Garfield books.